THE BALL BOOK

Modern Curriculum Press
**BEGINNING
TO
READ**
Series

THE
BALL BOOK

Margaret Hillert

Illustrated by Nan Brooks

Library of Congress Cataloging in Publication Data

Hillert, Margaret.
  The ball book.

  (MCP beginning-to-read books)
  Summary: People play a variety of games involving balls on the big ball that is Earth.
  [1. Ball games — Fiction.   2. Balls (Sporting goods) — Fiction.
3. Games — Fiction] I. Brooks, Nan.   II. Title.
PZ7.H558Bl   [E]   80-23590

ISBN 0-8136-5606-0 Paperback
ISBN 0-8136-5106-9 Hardbound

19 20   02 01

Balls, balls, balls.
Big balls. Little balls.
Balls for you and me.

I like balls.
I can play with this one.
I make it go up and down.

You can play with me.

Look out.

Here it comes.

Get it. Get it.

This is fun to play.
The ball is a little one.
Can you get this little ball?

Look at the little ones here.

Pretty little ones.

Make one go in.

Make one go out.

Here is a big ball.
You can jump on it.
Jump, jump, jump.

And here is one for the cat.
Something is in this little ball.
The cat will run and run to
get it.

This is a little ball, too.
I make it go.

You make it go.
We have fun with it.

You have to get this ball up.
Up, up, and in.
You have to work at it.
Work, work, work.

Now look at this ball.
You can make something go
down with it.
Down, down, down.

Good, good.
You did it!

You did it!
Good for you.

And this is fun, too.

You have to run, run, run
to get this ball.
Oh, my. Oh, my.

Father and Mother like to
play with this ball.

Look at it go.
Away, away it goes.

Look up, up, up.

Get this ball up.
Help it go.

This is good to play at school.
But you have to look out!
Look out for this ball.

Here is a funny ball.
Can you guess what it is for?
What can you do with it?

This is what you
do with it.
You run and run
and run.

We can play with this ball,
and we see it on TV.
We run and run with
this ball, too.

This ball is fun to play with.
You are good at this.
Mother and Father come to
see you play.

This is a big, big, BIG ball!
We are on this ball.
That is funny.

We work on it.
We play on it.

What a good ball it is!

Margaret Hillert, author of several books in the MCP Beginning-To-Read Series, is a writer, poet, and teacher.

The Ball Book uses the 62 words listed below.

a	get	make	that
and	go	me	the
are	goes	Mother	this
at	good	my	to
away	guess		too
		now	TV
ball(s)	have		
big	help	oh	up
but	here	on	
		one(s)	we
can	I	out	what
cat	in		will
come(s)	is	play	with
	it	pretty	work
did			
do	jump	run	you
down			
	like	school	
Father	little	see	
for	look	something	
fun			
funny			